DC COMICS™

BATMAN™

TALES OF THE

BATCAVE

DINO DEATH-TRAP

by
MICHAEL DAHL

illustrated by
LUCIANO VECCHIO

Batman created by
BOB KANE WITH BILL FINGER

Raintree is an imprint of Capstone Global Library Limited, a
company incorporated in England and Wales having its registered
office at 264 Banbury Road, Oxford, OX2 7DY – Registered company
number: 6695582

www.raintree.co.uk
myorders@raintree.co.uk

Text © Capstone Global Library Limited 2017
The moral rights of the proprietor have been asserted.

ISBN 978 1 4747 2913 0
20 19 18 17 16
10 9 8 7 6 5 4 3 2 1

British Library Cataloguing in Publication Data
A full catalogue record for this book is available from the British Library.

Every effort has been made to contact copyright holders of material reproduced in this book.
Any omissions will be rectified in subsequent printings if notice is given to the publisher.

All the internet addresses (URLs) given in this book were valid at the time of going to press.
However, due to the dynamic nature of the internet, some addresses may have changed, or
sites may have changed or ceased to exist since publication. While the author and publisher
regret any inconvenience this may cause readers, no responsibility for any such changes can
be accepted by either the author or the publisher.

Editor: Christopher Harbo
Designer: Bob Lentz
Production Specialist: Kathy McColley

Printed and bound in China.

Contents

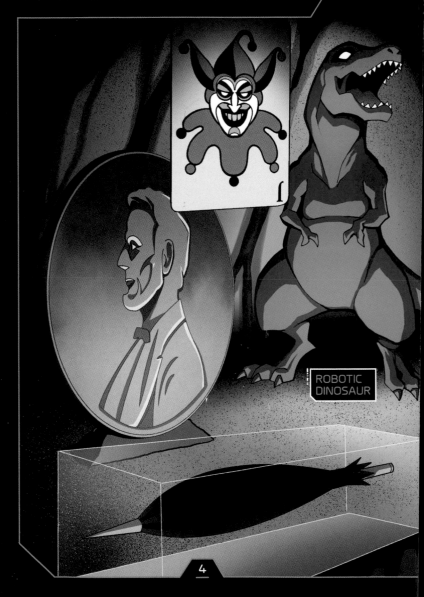

ROBOTIC DINOSAUR

It is the secret headquarters of Batman and his crime-fighting partner, Robin.

Hundreds of trophies, awards and souvenirs fill the Batcave's hidden rooms. Each one tells a story of danger, villainy and victory.

This is the tale of a robotic dinosaur! And why this trophy now stands in the Batcave . . .

CHAPTER 1

THE RIDDLE

Deep in the heart of Arkham Asylum prison, an alarm bell rings.

"The Riddler has escaped!" a guard cries.

"But how could he?" the governor asks.

He and the guard stand outside an empty prison cell.

"I don't know," says the guard. "The door is still locked."

"What is that?" says the governor, pointing.

A folded piece of paper lies on the bed.

The guard enters the cell and picks up the paper. "It's a riddle," he says.

The governor reads the message.

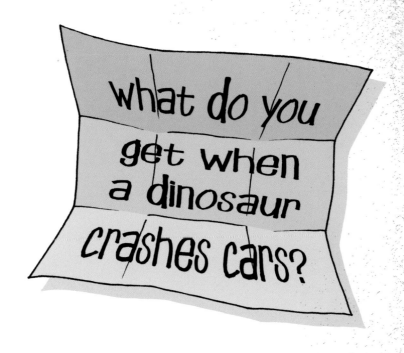

what do you get when a dinosaur crashes cars?

"What does it mean?" asks the guard.

"It means we need Batman and Robin," replies the governor. "Now!"

CHAPTER 2

SHADOWS IN THE MUSEUM

Dinosaur Island Amusement Park's prehistoric museum is closed for the night.

Two shadows move through the quiet rooms.

It is the Dark Knight and his partner Robin, the Boy Wonder.

"The answer to the riddle was easy," says Robin.

"What do you get when a dinosaur crashes cars?" he repeats. "You get Tyrannosaurus wrecks!"

Batman nods.

"And the only Tyrannosaurus in Gotham
City is in that room," he says.

He leads Robin to a huge room full of
dinosaur skeletons.

In the centre of the room stands a gigantic Tyrannosaurus rex.

The T. rex is not a normal skeleton like the others. It is a huge robot model of the prehistoric creature.

The dino robot stands 10 metres tall with eyes made of thick glass.

"Look, Batman!" shouts Robin.

Behind one of the glass eyes is a shadow.

The eye swings open like a window.

A man in a green suit and hat leans out and laughs!

It's the Riddler!

"Here's a riddle for you, Batman," says
the Riddler.

"When is a dinosaur like a chicken in the
hen house?" the Riddler laughs. "When they're
both a layer!"

"Layer? Oh, of course," says Robin. "Layer
sounds like lair. The dino is the Riddler's
lair – his hideout!"

CHAPTER 3

DEEP IN THE DINO

"Catch me if you can!" shouts the villain.

The heroes spy a door in the belly of the beast. They rush inside the giant dino.

CLANG!

The heavy door shuts behind them.

"It's locked!" cries Robin. "We're trapped!"

"Then the Riddler is trapped inside with us," says Batman.

HAHAHAHAHAHAHAHAHA!

Creepy laughter echoes inside the robot.

The heroes rush up a metal staircase, following the laughs. They climb to a round room inside the dino's head.

But the Riddler is gone. The laughter is coming from a speaker on the wall.

"That's right," says the voice. "I'm outside. And you are inside – a cell!"

The door to the round room shuts and locks.

"The walls and windows are made of a special plastic," says the voice. "Even the Dynamic Duo can't break through it."

Suddenly, Batman and Robin are thrown to
the floor.

"It's an earthquake!" shouts Robin.

"It's no earthquake," says Batman. "The dino is moving!"

"A very moving experience, indeed," crows the Riddler. "And your next stop – the bottom of Gotham City Harbour!"

The robot dino crashes through the wall of the museum.

CHAPTER 4

LOSING AIR

On and on the metal monster marches through the dark streets.

Soon it reaches the edge of Gotham City Harbour.

Robin stares out a dino-eye window. "It's not stopping!" he shouts.

The heroes hear a loud splash. The dino stomps into the dark water.

"I hope the dino doesn't crash into those boats," says Robin.

Batman is silent. He's using a cutting torch from his belt to cut through the wall.

"It's working," says Batman. "But not fast enough. By the time I cut through, we'll be out to sea. In deep water."

Robin examines the walls and the windows.

No way out, he thinks. But also, no way in.

No way for air to get into the room.

"Your cutting torch is using up the oxygen," says Robin.

"I know," says Batman. "But there's no other way out."

Robin checks the oxygen mask on his Utility Belt. It would help, but it couldn't last forever.

A beam of light flashes in the window.

"What's that?" asks Batman.

"One of the boats in the harbour," says Robin.

The Dark Knight jumps up and joins Robin at the eye-windows.

"Those lights," Batman says. "They're our new hope."

CHAPTER 5

A MOVEABLE BEAST

Batman grabs a torch from his belt. "Robin, use your light with me," he says.

The two heroes aim their torches out the windows.

"If we can attract the attention of one of the captains . . ." Batman begins, ". . . we could use Morse code!"

"Brilliant idea!" says the Boy Wonder. "Ships use it all the time to signal each other!"

The heroes' signal attracts three boats. They surround the marching dinosaur.

Metal grinds against metal as their hulls push against the beast.

Slowly, the boats turn the dino around.

"It's working, Batman!" cries Robin. "The dino is heading back towards shore!"

Meanwhile, back at the museum, the Riddler and his men grab their treasures.

"No one can stop us," the Riddler crows. "Fill your bags with loot!"

CRASSSHHHHHHH!!

The wall of the museum caves in. The dino
has returned!

The robot creature trips on the rubble and tips over.

WHOMP!

The Riddler and his men are stuck inside the metal jaws of the T. rex.

Batman and Robin have escaped their dino prison.

"Look, Batman," cries Robin. "The Riddler is tripped up with the treasure in his own trap."

"Nicely put, Boy Wonder," Batman says, smiling. "Yes, it's a case of the booty and the beast."

EPILOGUE . . .

"What should we do with the dino, Batman?"

"Let's take it to the Batcave, Boy Wonder."

"Why?"

"To honor our adventure in the belly of the beast."

Glossary

asylum hospital for people who are mentally ill

booty another name for treasure

cell small room with locks; some cells have bars

harbour place where ships can dock

lair secret place where a person hides out

layer chicken or other animal that lays eggs

Morse code system of signalling using dots and dashes sent as sound or light

oxygen colourless gas in the air that people and animals need to breathe

prehistoric from a time before history was recorded

souvenir object kept as a reminder of a person, place or event

Discuss

1. The Riddler uses a clever pun in one of his riddles. It is a pun because the two different words layer and lair sound the same. Do you know any good puns?

2. If Robin had been trapped inside the dino alone, would he have been able to escape? How did the two heroes work together to save themselves from ending up in the ocean?

3. Batman and Robin have special Utility Belts to help them fight crime. Can you name three items in their belts that are mentioned in this story?

Write

1. The Riddler used the robot dino as his secret hideout. Can you think of another good hideout for him? Describe where it is and how it looks.

2. Batman, Robin, and the Riddler all wear special uniforms. Describe a uniform that you would wear if you were a superhero or villain. Draw a picture of it.

3. Batman and Robin came up with a brilliant way of escaping an underwater doom. Write a paragraph explaining another way they could have escaped the dino and captured the Riddler.

Author

Michael Dahl is the prolific author of the best-selling *Goodnight Baseball* picture book and more than 200 other books for children and young adults. In the United States, he has won the AEP Distinguished Achievement Award three times for his non-fiction, a Teachers' Choice Award from *Learning* magazine, and a Seal of Excellence from the Creative Child Awards. He is also the author of the Hocus Pocus Hotel mystery series and the Dragonblood books. Dahl currently lives in Minneapolis, Minnesota, USA.

Illustrator

Luciano Vecchio was born in 1982 and is based in Buenos Aires, Argentina. Freelance artist for many projects at Marvel and DC Comics, his work has been seen in print and online around the world. He has illustrated many DC Super Heroes books for Capstone, and some of his recent comic work includes *Beware the Batman*, *Green Lantern: The Animated Series*, *Young Justice*, *Ultimate Spider-Man*, and his creator-owned web-comic, *Sereno*.